Say "Cheese"!

Written by Katie Foufouti

Illustrated by Rupert Van Wyk

Collins

What's in this story?

Listen and say 🎧①

taking photos

playing games

dancing

making noise

having fun

singing

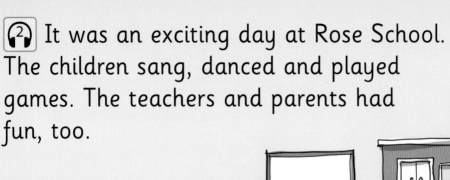 It was an exciting day at Rose School. The children sang, danced and played games. The teachers and parents had fun, too.

Ben took photos of everyone with his camera.

5

Miss Hill wanted a photo of Class 4A.
It wasn't easy. There were lots of children
and they made a lot of noise.

Quiet please,
children!

7

Ben was ready. The teacher was ready.
The children were ready.

Ben took the photo, but ...

... it wasn't a good photo.

Don't worry!
Let's try again.

Ben took another photo.

It was a better photo, but there was a bird in it. It was in front of Vicky, Tim and Lily.

Ben counted again, "*3 ... 2 ... 1 ... Cheese!*"
Was it a good photo this time?

Oh no! A basketball hit Ben's camera.
What a terrible photo! It was worse than
the other photos.

My camera!

The children were tired, but they really wanted a photo of this day. Ben said, "One last time, 3 … 2 … 1 … Chee …."

There was no photo. Everyone was sad. Then Micha had an idea. She ran to the classroom.

Micha looked on Miss Hill's desk. Where was it? Aha! She found it and ran back to her friends. What was it?

It was the class tablet. Micha held it up and was about to take a group selfie. Then she stopped. Who wasn't in the photo?

The children wanted Ben to be in the
photo, too.

Come here, Ben!

Everyone was ready.
Micha said, "3 … 2 … 1 …"
Everyone said, "Cheese!"

What a great photo! Well done, Micha!

Picture dictionary

Listen and repeat

basketball

battery

bird

camera

photo

selfie

tablet

1 Look and order the story

2 Listen and say

Collins

Published by Collins
An imprint of HarperCollins*Publishers*
Westerhill Road
Bishopbriggs
Glasgow
G64 2QT

HarperCollins*Publishers*
1st Floor, Watermarque Building
Ringsend Road
Dublin 4
Ireland

William Collins' dream of knowledge for all began with the publication of his first book in 1819.

A self-educated mill worker, he not only enriched millions of lives, but also founded a flourishing publishing house. Today, staying true to this spirit, Collins books are packed with inspiration, innovation and practical expertise. They place you at the centre of a world of possibility and give you exactly what you need to explore it.

© HarperCollins*Publishers* Limited 2020

10 9 8 7 6 5 4 3 2

ISBN 978-0-00-839832-3

Collins® and COBUILD® are registered trademarks of HarperCollins*Publishers* Limited

www.collins.co.uk/elt

British Library Cataloguing in Publication Data

A catalogue record for this publication is available from the British Library.

Author: Katie Foufouti
Illustrator: Rupert Van Wyk (Beehive)
Series editor: Rebecca Adlard
Publishing manager: Lisa Todd
Product managers: Jennifer Hall and Caroline Green
In-house editor: Alma Puts Keren
Project manager: Emily Hooton
Editor: Frances Amrani
Proofreaders: Natalie Murray and Michael Lamb
Cover designer: Kevin Robbins
Typesetter: 2Hoots Publishing Services Ltd
Audio produced by id audio, London
Reading guide author: Emma Wilkinson
Production controller: Rachel Weaver
Printed and bound by: GPS Group, Slovenia

Download the audio for this book and a reading guide for parents and teachers at www.collins.co.uk/839832